Walt Disney's

ELMER
ELEPHANT

This little book is dedicated to my millions of friends whose loyalty has been so helpful in my efforts to amuse the world

Walt Disney

WALT DISNEY'S
ELMER ELEPHANT

Plus
PECULIAR PENGUINS

DAVID McKAY COMPANY, INC.
New York

ELMER ELEPHANT

Copyright © 1934, 1936 by Walt Disney Productions

All rights reserved, including the right to
reproduce this book, or parts thereof, in any
form, except for the inclusion of brief
quotations in a review.

10 9 8 7 6 5 4 3 2 1

Library of Congress Cataloging Card Number: 78-19231

ISBN 0-679-20602-7

ELMER ELEPHANT

Elmer Elephant was going to a party. A birthday party for Tillie Tiger! He was so happy that he skipped and danced through the forest—ka-thunk ka-thump ka-thunk ka-thump—in his funny, clumsy, little-boy-elephant way.

For a present he was bringing Tillie a bouquet of the brightest and gayest flowers in the whole forest. With the tip of his soft trunk, he would nose out the prettiest ones and pick them.

ELMER ELEPHANT

Soon he came to the high fence that surrounded Tillie's home. Shouts of laughter from the inside told him that most of the guests had arrived and that the party had already started. So he opened the gate and peeked inside.

Tillie saw him at once and called "Hurry, Elmer. You're just in time. I'm going to blow out the candles on my cake!"

ELMER ELEPHANT

Elmer ran forward and stood at one end of the table. It was the end nearest Tillie. It was also the end nearest the cake.

"Now—watch me!" cried Tillie, and she drew in a great breath of air. Then she blew—very, VERY hard. But the candles merely flickered, as if they were winking at her.

Again she tried. This time she filled her cheeks with so much air she looked like a fat squirrel with a mouthful of nuts. But again the candles only winked, as if they were laughing to themselves.

ELMER ELEPHANT

Elmer Elephant was sure he could blow them all out, and he hoped Tillie would ask him. But instead she called to Joey Hippopotamus.

"You do it, Joey," she said. "You're so much stronger than I am."

"Well, of course, if you insist," said Joey proudly. And he swaggered up to the table.

Looking very important, Joey threw back his head and drew in a tremendous breath of air. And then——he B L E W !

ELMER ELEPHANT

In fact, he blew so hard that the birthday cake flew up in the air and came down skwush! right on top of Elmer Elephant. And the words "Happy Birthday" were spattered all over his face.

There was a sudden hush. Then you should have heard the shrieks of laughter! All the children clapped their hands and shouted.

"Look at Elmer!"

"Happy Birthday, Elmer!"

"Yoo-hoo! Happy Birthday! Ha ha ha ha!"

ELMER ELEPHANT

Elmer Elephant just stood there. He was too surprised to move.

Tillie ran forward and told him not to mind. She'd have him fixed up in no time. And she did, too, for she wiped off every last bit of the cake and frosting.

Not until then did Elmer remember the flowers he had brought. And when he handed them to her, Tillie was so pleased she gave him a big kiss, right on top of his trunk.

ELMER ELEPHANT

Elmer was terribly embarrassed. His face turned a deep, dark red. But he was so happy he almost burst!

This made the others jealous, so they started to tease Elmer. Tillie stopped them for a moment by saying there was more cake in her house, and she would go up and get it.

ELMER ELEPHANT

Elmer stood watching her so he did not notice all the other boys gathering together, whispering. The first thing he knew was when one of them knocked into him, and then another, and still another. One had a long stem hanging from his nose, another had a stocking and a third had a piece of garden hose. And all waddled by with a slow, swinging walk, just like Elmer's.

ELMER ELEPHANT

The little elephant could not understand it. He knew they were making fun of him. But why should they? And why did they hold those long stems and socks up to their noses? He just couldn't figure it out.

Then one of the boys caught him by his trunk and gave it a jerk. When he let go, another grabbed his trunk and jerked it. Elmer tried to defend himself, but there were too many to fight all at once. Finally they backed him clear out of Tillie's yard and away from the party. Then they leaned over the fence and yelled at him.

ELMER ELEPHANT

Poor Elmer! He tried to be brave and not cry. But it is hard to be brave when you find that other boys don't like you. Especially when they dislike you so much they chase you away from a party where you are having fun.

Feeling very sorry for himself, Elmer walked through the forest, till he came to his favorite pool. He thought the cold water would soothe his aching trunk and make him feel better.

ELMER ELEPHANT

To-day the pool was so clear it shone like a mirror. Elmer flung himself down and looked into the cool depths, trying to think of some reason why the boys had made fun of him. Then his eyes opened wide. He shook his head and looked again.

As many times as he had bathed in the pool, the little elephant boy had never stopped to look at himself. For the first time in his life he saw the reflection of his trunk. He was perfectly used to the feel of it, but he had never seen it before as others saw it.

Horrors! Was THIS his nose! Then no wonder the boys had made fun of him. Why, no one in the forest had such a long nose. Not one!

ELMER ELEPHANT

The longer Elmer Elephant looked, the longer his nose seemed to be! Something had to be done. He must get rid of it, somehow. He tried to tuck it down inside his blouse, but as soon as he looked up, it popped out again. He tried to roll it up, but it came unrolled. He even tied a knot in it. But that made him look worse than ever.

His lip quivered. Tears streamed down his cheeks. He knew it was no use. He had that awful nose, and he had to keep it. And wherever he went, people would ALWAYS poke fun at him.

ELMER ELEPHANT

Suddenly he heard a voice that seemed to come from high in the air. Looking up quickly, Elmer saw his friend, the Giraffe.

"What's the matter, son?" asked old Caleb. "Havin' nose trouble?"

Elmer blinked the tears away, sniffed a bit, and nodded his head.

"Well, now, that's too bad," said the Giraffe. "But don't you mind. People used to laugh at my long neck, too. But they soon stopped when they saw me eatin' the tender top leaves of the trees that they couldn't reach themselves! An' what's more, long noses are sometimes just as useful as long necks.

"For instance, just look at those birds over there," he continued. "If their beaks aren't funnier than your nose, I'll swallow my spots an' eat my whiskers."

Looking around, Elmer saw three great, clumsy pelicans with huge pouches hanging from their long beaks.

"Those beaks are funny-lookin'," Caleb went on, "but they're mighty handy. When pelicans are fishin', they wouldn't trade their beaks for the prettiest noses in the world. And do you think they care if other birds laugh at 'em? Not a bit! They just sit there, an' smile to themselves, an' eat the fish those beaks helped 'em catch."

ELMER ELEPHANT

All at once old Caleb stopped speaking and began to sniff the air excitedly.

"I smell smoke," he said. Then, rearing up his long neck, he looked all around. His neck was as tall as a tower, so he could see a long, long distance. And what he saw made him tremble with fear.

"It's Tillie's house," he sputtered. "Tillie Tiger's house is afire!"

Elmer jumped up. He forgot his nose. He forgot the pelicans. He forgot the boys who had made fun of him. He forgot everything except that Tillie was in danger. And he must do something to help save her.

ELMER ELEPHANT

He started running, as fast as his stubby legs would carry him. As he ran, he had to make way for the Fire Chief, who was driving a bright red ostrich-cart. The Chief was followed by the jungle fire engine, dashing madly through the forest, with the monkey firemen hanging on for dear life. Long after it had passed, Elmer could hear its sirens wailing and screaming.

Fire! Fire! Tillie's house was on fire! And Elmer's feet went pound, pound, pounding through the jungle. He had to be there in time.

ELMER ELEPHANT

Just as his breath gave out and he feared he would never make it, Elmer felt himself lifted high in the air. At first, he was startled. Then he saw what had happened. His friend, the Giraffe, had hoisted him up on his long neck. Now they were fairly whizzing along. And in almost no time, they were there.

Fire was blazing all around the floor of Tillie's house. Little flames were licking the grass walls. The wooden steps leading up the pole had burned away. Tillie was trapped. No ladder was long enough to reach her. No hose could shoot water so high. It seemed that no one could help her.

ELMER ELEPHANT

Elmer looked around. He was almost frantic. Then he saw the three pelicans. He called to them to bring some water. They flew to a nearby stream, dove down, and filled their huge beaks.

Elmer balanced himself on the giraffe's head. And as the pelicans flew by, he dipped his trunk into their pouches and took a deep breath. Then, turning around, he shot the water at the flames.

ELMER ELEPHANT

Down below, the crowd began to take heart and cheer. But Elmer did not hear them. He had but one thought. Water. More water. Another pelican. Another trunkful of water. Another swhish-h-h-h! as it splashed against the burning house.

Elmer's trunk—the trunk the boys had laughed at—was the only thing that could save Tillie, and it WAS saving her.

ELMER ELEPHANT

For soon—the fire began to die down. Elmer was gaining on it. But he could still hear Tillie calling to him. And, with victory in sight, he worked harder than ever.

With the last trunkful of water, Elmer turned toward the house. Then he hesitated. He stopped. He blinked. There was no place to shoot the water. The fire was out!

Elmer Elephant sighed with relief. He had won. He had saved Tillie. But he shot the last trunkful, anyway—just to be sure.

ELMER ELEPHANT

Then Old Caleb stretched his neck up as far as he possibly could. Elmer reached out and gently lifted Tillie down. And, very slowly, Old Caleb lowered both of them to the ground.

Now, the forest folk were wild with excitement. They shouted and cheered, and waved their hats.

ELMER ELEPHANT

Tillie thanked Old Caleb and the three brave pelicans. Then she ran back to Elmer Elephant.

"You're a hero, Elmer," she told him. "A really truly hero. You saved my life."

Elmer kicked the ground with his foot. His big ears burned from so much praise. But he was happy again, for he knew that Tillie really did like him.

ELMER ELEPHANT

And no one thought of making fun of Elmer Elephant's nose now. Indeed not! He was the hero of the hour, and the other boys would have given their ears, their tails and their own stubby noses to be in his place. Especially when Tillie gave him another kiss. A great big one, this time!

So, after that, Elmer Elephant never worried about his long trunk again. He just loved it. And so did Tillie. And so do I!

PECULIAR PENGUINS

Way down at the South Pole End of the world
live the Penguins. Yes, as far South as the North
wind can blow and the sea gulls can go lies Penguin
Island.

The sea gulls have gone there again and again,
But the Penguins themselves are like queer little
  men,
And their Island's so snowy and blowy and gay
It's merry as Christmas down there every day!

How those Penguins can coast! How those Penguins
can slide!

Go fishing and swimming and out for a ride

On a nice cake of ice, you would think they would
freeze,

For it's colder than cold in those old Polar Seas.

But the Penguins don't mind it, those fellows, I'm told

Never freeze, never sneeze—never even catch cold!

Their feathers fit so close and snug they keep warm
even when Jack Frost himself is blowing on his fingers.
And you have no idea what a jolly life they lead on

their rocky little island with their coasting, swimming, fishing and birthday parties!

Every time a Penguin has a birthday there is a big frosted cake with icicle candles, and there are SO many Penguins there are simply hundreds of birthday parties. That is why Penguins wear their birthday clothes all the time, the Gentlemen Penguins and boys, white shirts and black tail coats, the Lady Penguins and little girls, white feathered bibs and black tuckers. No wonder they step around proudly with their chests stuck up and their toes pointing east and west. They're proud of wearing their best clothes every day; proud

of their wings, too! For Penguins have water wings and are the only birds in the world who cannot fly.

Having wings for the water and not for the air
Makes Penguins peculiar, unusual and rare,
At home on the sea and at home on the land,
These peculiar young Penguins think life is just grand!

And while the Mother Penguins sit high on the rocks teaching the children their A, B, seas and the old Chiefs march up and down the shore telling of the fish they've caught in their youth, how high they

can dive and stay under water without coming up for air, and the proper way to swallow an eel or boil an icicle—the YOUNG Penguins are out doing all these exciting things.   Going

> Flipper flapper, slipper slapper ZIP
> Down icy slides,
> Turning somersaults and wintersaults
> And upside down besides!

And of all the young Penguins, none had a better time than Peter.   But Peter was never happy unless

Polly Penguin was along. Peter thought Polly the most beautiful bird on the island. He just could not look at her enough. Polly liked to look at herself, for that matter, and did it quite often,

> For the ice made mirrors fine and clear
> So Polly's glass was always near,
> And just by glancing in the ice
> She'd see if she were looking nice.

Polly looked so very nice to Peter he spent all his time trying to please her, bringing her bright shells for

necklaces, strands of sea weed for belts and fat little
fish to tempt her appetite.

And so long as there were only Penguins about,
Polly was glad enough to go swimming and fishing
with Peter or have him pick her ripe ice cream cones.

> Ice *cream* cones really grow there
> On that island, sweet as any—
> Icicle cones, with snow ice cream,
> That do not cost a penny!

And there you are! But just as Polly and Peter
would settle down for a jolly time together, along

would come Wally Walrus and he spoiled everything for Peter.

Wally was so big and handsome and he talked in such a loud barking voice, Polly thought he must know everything and be about the strongest fellow in the world. No matter WHAT Peter did, Wally could do the same thing better. He could swim faster, sing louder, throw a ball farther and even beat Peter at his own game of Penguin tenpins. It was *all* so discouraging.

But one frosty morning, Peter set out quite happily to find her. This time he was sure he had a present that would please her. He had got up while it was still

dark to make her a snow sled and as he hurried along
he thought what a fine time he'd have pulling Polly
over the ice.

Polly scarcely looked at the handsome sled when
Peter swung it round for her to see, but Wally's eyes
simply snapped with interest and envy. Not having any
present for Polly himself, he decided to use Peter's sled.

"Come along Polly! Let's go aquaplaning!" he
bellowed and snatching the rope of the sled from Peter
he tumbled into the sea.

By the time Peter had recovered from his surprise
they had both disappeared in a flying spray of sea
water.

"Bring back my sled, you big Marine! Oh, how can Polly be so mean?" groaned Peter. Then, whistling to keep from getting too mad, he began to make a big snow ball. "Won't Polly be surprised when she sees this!" he thought, thumping ·and pounding it into shape.

But when Polly and Wally presently came puffing back to shore, Polly was not surprised at all. She just sniffed at Peter's snow ball.

"Call that a snow ball?" whooped Wally, and with a few sweeps of his powerful flippers he rolled up a snow ball as big as himself.

"What do you think of that, my little Penguin?" he asked, standing back to admire his own work.

"Pretty good for a start and for a Walrus, but wait here and I'll show you a real one," said Peter dashing up a hill that lay just ahead.

> "It *is* not always strength that counts,
>   Some cleverness and skill
>   Will often win the day.   Hurray,
>   I know a few tricks still,"

hummed Peter as he hurried up the icy incline. Starting at the top with a little snow ball he pushed it carefully ahead of him. As it rolled down it grew

bigger and bigger and bigger and by the time it reached the bottom was *so* enormous, it made Wally's snow ball look like a tiny sugar pill.

"Oh Peter, what a beautiful snow ball!" cried Polly turning her back on Wally. "How strong you must be!"

And that was one time Peter Penguin got the best of Wally Walrus. But while he stood twirling his cap and smiling at Polly a loud voice came booming down from the hill and there was Wally on the very top of a long slippery slide.

"Look, Polly! Watch me dive!" he bawled jeal-

ously and as Polly and Peter turned to look, he came swooping down and shot gracefully out over the water in a perfect tusk over tail spin.

Forgetting all about the splendid snow ball Peter had made her, Polly danced up and down shouting with pleasure and excitement, and turning angrily away, Peter rushed up the hill himself. He'd show Polly how a slide and dive really should be done. Wally might be heavier, but he knew a few things about flapping his wings as he coasted down that would send him much farther than Wally had gone. As Wally came panting ashore wearing a grin that

reached all the way back to his ears, Peter gave a whoop and started down:

> Helter skelter-pelter PLOP
> As if he never meant to stop!

And when Wally saw the way Peter's wings were helping him along and realized that Peter was going to beat him at high diving too, he gave a spiteful kick that sent a heap of rocks and sand flying into Peter's path. Polly had her eyes fixed earnestly on Peter and did not see Wally's sly trick. Peter saw

him, though, but it was already too late. When he reached the foot of the hill, instead of sailing high out over the water he came to such a sharp stop he stubbed his bill on a rock and scraped most of the feathers off his chest.

Prickling all over with rage and disappointment, Peter bounced up to tell Wally what he thought of such behavior, when just ahead, peering up out of the water he saw an even worse enemy. The worst and most deadly enemy a Penguin can have. At the same moment a dozen voices called warningly "SHARK! SHARK!"

"Shark! Shark!" Immediately the cry was taken up by all the others and from every direction Penguins came flocking down to the edge of the island. In the water the shark swam in sulky circles, gnashing his teeth and blinking his fierce little eyes at the plump bodies of the Penguins and the still plumper body of the Walrus.

Shuddering to think how nearly he had fallen into the monster's mouth, Peter hurried up to Wally and shook him warmly by the flipper. Good, honest generous little Peter thought Wally had seen the shark and kicked sand and stones in the path to save

his life. Of course, Wally had not seen the shark, but it was pleasant to be considered a hero and Wally took all the praise and pats on the back with a pleased grin.

However, with a shark just off shore, the Penguins could not waste time even for a hero and blowing on a conch shell Old Chief Elder Penny called a council of the Chiefs. Sitting in a solemn circle they decided it was not safe for anyone to swim, dive or play in the ocean at all. So a stern order to stay on the island was sent out to the whole Penguin band.

While the old Chiefs sat 'round the council fire, most of the young Penguins settled down to quiet

games ashore. Polly was sitting on the edge of a pool, watching a game of water ball when Wally Walrus came blustering up.

"My! My! How dull it is to-day," grunted Wally shifting from one flipper to the other. "Are you going to sit here all day doing nothing? Let's go swimming or have a good game of sea tag!"

"But what about the shark?" whispered Polly, looking nervously over her shoulder. "And you know very well we were forbidden to leave the island."

"Pooh, that's all right for a few scary Penguins, but nobody can frighten me!" barked Wally:

"If that shark shows his ugly nose
   I'll give it such a tweak
   He'll soon turn tail—I never fail
   To make such monsters squeak!"

And seizing Polly's wing he hurried her down to the beach.

Polly knew she should not go. But the sea, cold and sparkling blue under the Polar sun looked so tempting, she longed for a good swim. And what could happen to her with a great fellow like Wally Walrus along?

But as they reached the water's edge, hurrying foot-steps came pattering behind them.

"Polly! Polly!" cried a sharp voice, "Don't go

out there. Do you wish to be eaten alive? What in feathers are you thinking of?"

Polly knew quite well what she was thinking of, but pretending not to hear Peter hurried on. That old shark was probably miles away by this time and it was foolish to waste the whole day on the island.

"Well—if it isn't Peter Penguin turning up like a bad penny," snorted Wally, flouncing round with a mocking grin. "What do you want now, you meddling little rock hopper?"

"I want Polly to come straight back with me," said Peter, too worried to care what Wally called him. "If you wish to go swimming with a shark, that's your own affair, but you shan't take Polly!"

"Oh shan't I?" roared Wally bristling his whiskers

fiercely. "How about it, Polly, will you stay here with Peter or come swimming with me?" Polly had already made up her mind. Though Peter did his best to stop her, though he got down on his Penguin knees and begged her not to go, she foolishly followed the Walrus into the water.

"Ho ho!" sputtered Wally. "Isn't this fun? I'll beat you to that cake of ice, my girl!" He did, too, but Polly didn't mind, for when she grew tired of swimming, Wally helped her up on the ice block and pushed her rapidly through the water with his powerful flippers.

It was so pleasant spinning over the surface of the sea, Polly forgot all about the shark, and Peter watching unhappily from the beach saw them going farther and farther away. Ruffling up his feathers, Peter ran distractedly up and down the sand—trying to think of some way to bring Polly to her senses or prove to her that Wally was not so brave as he pretended to be. Suddenly Peter struck his foot on a sharp sea shell and at the same time hit upon the very idea he was looking for.

"Hah!" cried Peter. Snatching up the shell, he broke off one side, tucked it under his wing and taking

a long breath, jumped into the ocean. Neither Wally nor Polly had seen Peter leave the Island and as he swam toward them under water they were lazily trying to decide what to do next. Wally was tired of pushing the ice block, and with Polly, sitting cozily in the center, it was drifting along beside him. Every now and then he would give it a gentle shove. But HORRORS! As he reached up to give it another poke, he saw the horrid striped fin of a shark sticking out of the water.

"Skyenwater!" choked Wally falling back tail over flippers. "Help! Help! Shark! The shark!" And

without even thinking of Polly he went streaking for shore blubbering and crying like a big frightened baby. Poor Polly! She could scarcely believe her eyes! But here was the shark coming nearer and nearer every minute and there was that good-for-nothing Walrus going farther and farther away. As she made ready to leap off the ice cake, Peter quietly stuck his head out of the water. He still had the shell under his wing and his eyes were twinkling with mischief at the way his plan had succeeded.

"Hello there!" laughed Peter. "Well—I certainly fooled Wally *that* time. He thought I was the shark

and there goes the big brave old sea lion yelping like a puppy. Suppose it had been the real shark, think what would have happened to you then!" But Polly did not have a chance to think, for just as they were chuckling over her lucky escape, there was a swish and swirl in the water ahead and this time it WAS the real shark. And he was coming straight for her.

"Don't move!" quavered Peter. "Stay right where you are," and flipping over backwards he began slapping the water with his wings and tumbling over and over like a porpoise. Peter was trying to make the shark chase him, so Polly would have time to swim to

shore. And as usual, Peter's plan worked. The shark distracted from the plump little Penguin right under his nose by the terrible commotion Peter was making —immediately set after him.

> The gulls flew left, the gulls flew right,
> As the shark with mighty slashes
> Cut through the waves. With all his might
> Poor Peter swims and splashes.

"Oh Peter, Peter, what will you do?" wailed Polly wringing her wings frantically, and they were wet enough to wring, goodness knows!

"Trust me!" called Peter, scrambling up on another cake of ice just a pin feather ahead of the enemy. His voice shook in spite of his brave words and *no* wonder! The little island of ice was too small to be of much use to him.

Indeed, in his first attempt to get at Peter, the shark bit off more than half of it and for several minutes continued to take frightful bites out of the edges. Eating his way toward the provoking young Penguin seemed a good idea, then, as the chilly ice made his teeth ache, he gave that up, and began chasing Peter viciously from side to side.

His eyes snapped with greed and impatience and at each turn he hoped Peter would slip into the water. But Peter was an expert on ice and no matter how fast he went somehow kept his balance.

So next the shark swam under the ice cake and humped his back, trying to spill Peter off that way. Peter went up, and Peter went down, and when the shark stuck his head out of the water there he was still sitting on the cake of ice.

And because that old shark didn't like Penguins on ice any more than some people like eggs on toast, he gave Peter's raft a terrific whack with his nose. Then he opened his mouth and waited for Peter to

fall in. But instead, the block of ice turned completely over and crashed down so hard on his ugly head, for a long moment he lay perfectly still. By the time he had shaken it off, Peter was away and swimming for dear life. A few miles to the east lay the palace of the Snow King and Peter was heading straight for the King's Island. There he would be safe from a thousand sharks and the King whom he had once done a service, would not only give him a hearty welcome, but would find some way to deal with this devouring monster, besides.

Now, while Peter pluckily pushed toward the east,

always managing to keep a bit of water between himself and the shark, Wally Walrus reached shore and pulling himself up on the rocks went flapping across the island.

"Shark! Shark!" croaked Wally bursting in upon the old Chiefs' Council of war. "Quick, come quick, he's after Peter and Polly." Then, without stopping to explain he turned and scuffled wildly back to the beach, followed by the whole Penguin band. The blood of the Old Chiefs' froze in their veins at the awful sight that met their eyes. Even the young Penguins shivered and shook in their feathers and

it takes a LOT to make these Polar birds shiver.
But that shark WAS a lot, enough to make the
bravest heart turn cold, and Polly, miserably marooned
on her cake of ice shivered and shook more than all
the rest!

Polly knew that if anything dreadful happened to
Peter and herself it would all be her own fault. Clasp-
ing and unclasping her flippers she watched Peter turn,
twist, dive over and under the shark itself, in an effort
to tire out, or completely bewilder his relentless pur-
suer. And all the time Peter was drawing the shark
farther and farther away from Polly. Knowing he

meant to save her, even if he could not save himself, Polly felt sorrier than ever. Only the block of ice she was standing on kept her from sinking with shame and remorse.

Peter was ready to sink himself from weariness and fatigue. His well thought-out plan for reaching the Snow King's Island had come to nought, for the shark making a savage turn had sent him fleeing in an entirely different direction. Now there was nothing ahead but the wide open sea—nothing behind but the wide open mouth of the shark and nothing for him to do but keep going. So Peter kept going expecting every moment to be his last.

Shading their eyes with their wings, the anxious band on Penguin Island viewed with growing dismay the thrilling race between Peter and the shark.

"He can't keep that pace up for ever," gasped old Chief Elder clutching his fur robe closely about him. "And when he stops, what will happen?" No one dared answer this dismal question, but everyone present had a good idea of what really would happen to poor brave little Peter Penguin.

Polly, out on her lonely island could not bear to look any more. Why, oh why had she not stayed ashore as Peter had begged her to do? Why had she ever followed that cowardly Walrus into the sea?

Peter's only hope was that the shark would tire out before he did, but considering its great size and the lively way it was still slashing through the water, this seemed hardly possible.

Indeed, tiring out the shark was such a long and breathless business, Peter began to puff and pant with exhaustion. No matter how fast he swam, or dived or turned in his tracks, he could feel the cold breath of the shark on his neck and hear its frightful scissor teeth snapping the water at his heels. Almost ready to give up the struggle, Peter made a despairing dive under an iceberg that happened to be floating by.

Like a blue streak the shark was after him, but misjudging the distance, he dashed against the ice, giving his nose such a knock it turned up ever afterward. Churning the water to a foam with his tail the furious fish looked savagely around for Peter.

There was not a sign of him anywhere, and blinking and snorting the shark whirled round like a top trying to discover which direction he had taken. Hah! There he was, the whole length of the iceberg away, too. But when he finally caught up, Peter had not only recovered his breath, but was all ready and waiting with a long icicle he had broken off the under side of the iceberg.

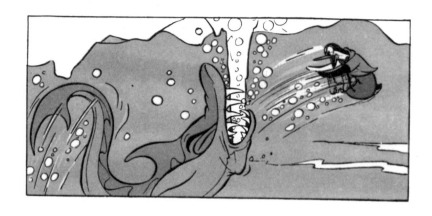

The shark's eyes were still watering from the blow he had got on the nose and without seeing the sharp weapon he made an open mouthed rush. Jamming the icicle down the shark's throat, Peter jumped aside.

Then, without waiting to see how he enjoyed his unexpected refreshments, Peter made off. Sure that the icicle would keep the shark busy for a little time anyway, Peter swam out from under the iceberg and rose breathlessly to the surface of the sea.

Now, if ever, was the right time for Polly to make a dash for safety and anxiously Peter began to wave to her with both wings. The shark was still under

water and catching Peter's frantic signal, Polly, without losing an instant, dove into the sea.

The sight of her going wing over flipper for shore, gave Peter new strength and courage to continue the fight and when the shark, choking with ice and indigestion, again came charging toward him, he began to swim around and round the iceberg as if he were wound up to go only in circles. Round and round and round went Peter and round and round and round went the shark, till the Penguins on the island could not tell whether the shark was chasing Peter or Peter was chasing the shark.

At times, even the shark was not sure, but closing

his eyes he kept grimly on, consoling himself with the thought of what he would do once he had caught this wretched little Penguin. His teeth would properly punish the saucy fellow for this maddening chase and when he had eaten him down to the last feather, he would go after the other one and eat her, too!

But the iceberg was not large and swimming in such small circles soon made the hungry sea beast so dizzy he did not know whether he was going east or west. This is what Peter wanted to happen. Glancing over his shoulder and making sure that Polly was safely ashore, Peter gave a great leap out of the water, landing on the iceberg with both wings round a big column of ice in the center.

The shark went half way round before he could stop, then giddy as a goat, he too hurled himself out of the water. As he struck, the iceberg rocked and tossed like a ship in a Nor'easter. When it finally stopped, and Peter could bring himself to look there lay his mighty enemy stretched cold and senseless at his feet. Cracking his head on the icy pillar he had knocked himself perfectly silly.

Thanking his lucky stars for such a stroke of good fortune, Peter looked down at his fallen foe. He even waited a moment longer to be sure that it could not stir.

Then, with a calm wave at his comrades on shore, Peter slid down the pole. Not caring to run any more races with the miserable monster, he bound him to the icy stake with strands of sea weed he fished out of the water. He had never tied up a shark before, but in spite of the creature's awkward size and shape he made a good and thorough job of it.

"There, that will hold him, for a little while anyway," sighed Peter and diving off the iceberg he swam thankfully back to Penguin Island. Now most chaps would have been satisfied with such a day's work, but

not Peter, first class, able bodied little sea-man that he was! Peter knew the effects of the blow would wear off, that the shark would jerk loose and be deadly and dangerous as ever for any Penguin bold enough to venture into the sea. Holding up his wing to stop the cheers with which his comrades welcomed him, Peter quickly explained a plan that had occurred to him while he was swimming ashore.

On the other side of Penguin Island lay the wreck of an old sailing vessel and with the entire flock trailing along, Peter made his way to this long abandoned old ship. Gaily Peter climbed aboard and with the

willing help of his mates ripped off the largest of the vessel's sails. They also took a big coil of rope. Then Peter and four strong young Penguins carried the sail and rope back to the beach and while those on shore watched in breathless interest, they swam out to the shark.

The once slashing thrashing old sea-wolf still lay like a stone on the ice. So, working as fast as they could, Peter and his sea-mates rigged up the sail and in less than the shake of a shirt had made a good sea-going vessel of the iceberg. There was a stiff breeze blowing from the North that filled out the sail almost

at once and bounding and plunging like a sea horse, Peter's ship with its strange cargo got under way!

"Sail along, old shark, without a crew—
    And shiver my flippers! When you come to
    You'll be a thousand miles away!
    And a long long voyage to you to-day!"

yelled Peter, dropping off the iceberg. The others jumped to, and away before the wind flew the shark's ship, so swiftly it was soon no more than a speck on the sky line. And they never saw fin, tooth nor tail of that shark again.

But Peter was the Hero of the hour. On the shoulders of two stalwart Penguins he was carried clear 'round the island with the whole Penguin band cheering and shouting behind him. No one even SAW Wally Walrus and shuffling enviously along on the edge of the crowd he was mad and miserable enough to chew clam shells. Polly would not look at him any more and it served him right. No, it was not hard to tell whom Polly thought the bravest now.

And after the grand celebration was over, and she and Peter were alone at last, Polly thanked him again for saving her life, thanked him with ALL her heart

and promised to marry him besides. So, marry they did, and lived happily even afterward on fish, frosted cake and snow pudding.   Think of it!

> That's the story of our Hero,
> Little Peter Penguineero,
> And his frozen Island in the Polar Sea!
> Where the days are cold and snappy
> And the Penguins cold and happy,
> Just as cozy cold and happy as can be!